Franklin Is Bossy

For the Pal family, especially Katie,
Charles and Stephanie, because
they love stories — PB

To Kerri Allen, a really good sport
— BC

Franklin is a trade mark of Kids Can Press Ltd.

Text copyright © 1993 by P.B. Creations Inc.
Illustrations copyright © 1993 by Brenda Clark Illustrator Inc.

We acknowledge the support of the Canada Council for the Arts
and the Ontario Arts Council for our publishing program.

Kids Can Press Ltd.
29 Birch Avenue
Toronto, Ontario, Canada
M4V 1E2

Book design by Michael Solomon and Brenda Clark
Typeset by Canadian Composition Inc.

Printed in Hong Kong by Wing King Tong Co. Ltd.

CDN PA 93 0 9 8 7 6

Canadian Cataloguing in Publication Data

Bourgeois, Paulette
  Franklin is bossy

ISBN   1-55074-119-5 (bound)   ISBN   1-55074-257-4 (pbk.)

1. Picture books for children.   I. Clark, Brenda.   II. Title.

PS8553.087F7   1993   jC813'.54   C93-093314-1
PZ7.B68F7   1993

Franklin Is Bossy

Written by Paulette Bourgeois
Illustrated by Brenda Clark

Kids Can Press

FRANKLIN the turtle could zip zippers and button buttons. He could count by twos and tie his shoes. He had lots of friends and one best friend, named Bear. They played tag and marbles, hopscotch and ball. But one day something awful happened. Franklin and Bear had a fight.

It was a steamy summer morning. Franklin told his friends, "Let's play marbles." And they did.

After a while, Franklin said, "I'm tired of marbles, let's have a race."

"You always pick the games," grumbled Bear.
Franklin paid no attention.
They started to run. Bear was in the lead.
Goose followed close behind. Franklin saw that he
was losing and cried out ...

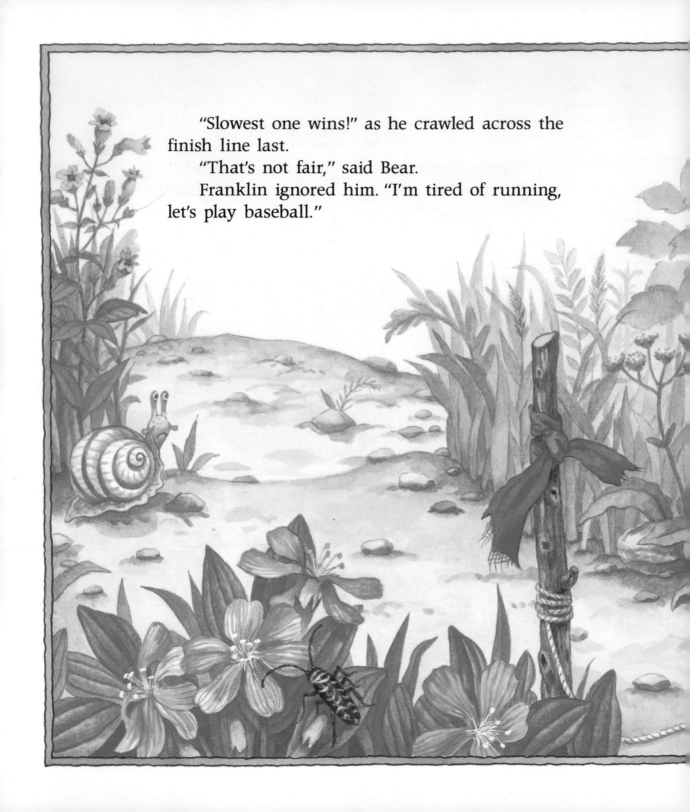

"Slowest one wins!" as he crawled across the finish line last.

"That's not fair," said Bear.

Franklin ignored him. "I'm tired of running, let's play baseball."

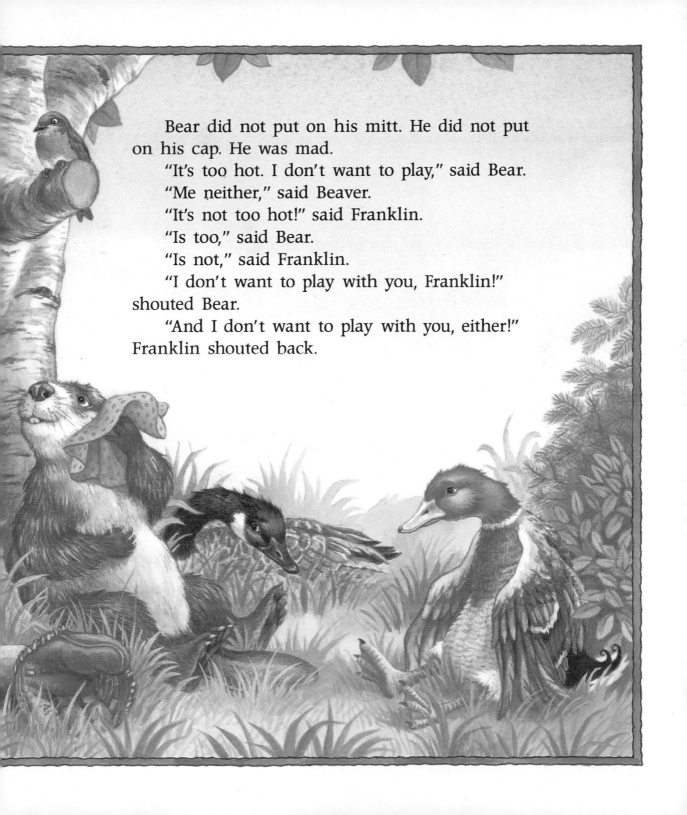

Bear did not put on his mitt. He did not put on his cap. He was mad.

"It's too hot. I don't want to play," said Bear.

"Me neither," said Beaver.

"It's not too hot!" said Franklin.

"Is too," said Bear.

"Is not," said Franklin.

"I don't want to play with you, Franklin!" shouted Bear.

"And I don't want to play with you, either!" Franklin shouted back.

Franklin stomped all the way home.

"What's wrong?" asked his father.

"There's no one to play with," answered
Franklin.

"Maybe your friends will come by later," said
Franklin's father.

"Maybe," he said.

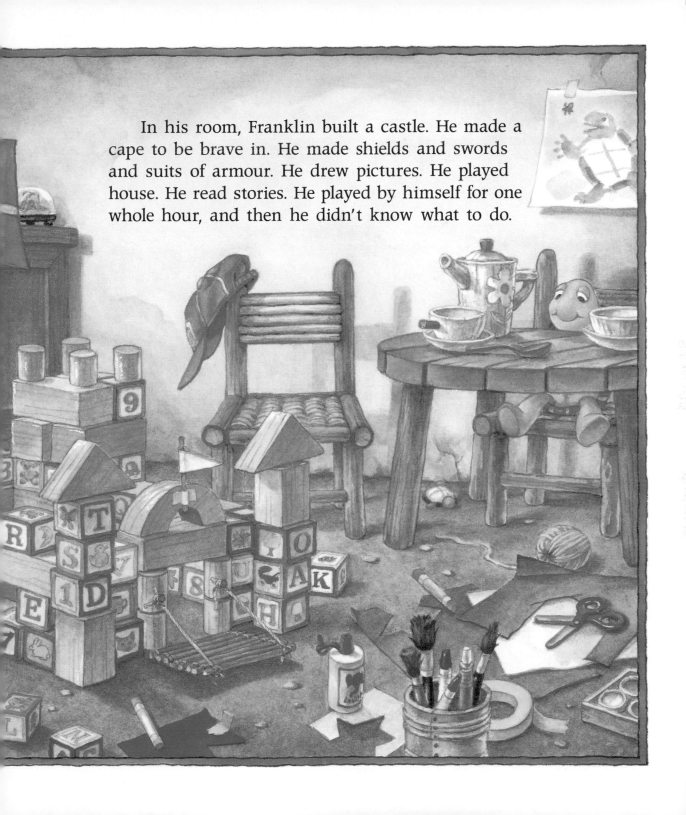

In his room, Franklin built a castle. He made a
cape to be brave in. He made shields and swords
and suits of armour. He drew pictures. He played
house. He read stories. He played by himself for one
whole hour, and then he didn't know what to do.

So, Franklin went looking for company.
His friends were in the river, cooling off.
"Are you still hot?" he asked.
"No," they answered.
"Then let's play ball," said Franklin.

Before anyone had a chance to say a word, Franklin started giving orders. "Bear, you play first base. Goose and Beaver, you go to the outfield. I'll be the pitcher."

"No way!" shouted Bear. "I don't want to play with you. You are too bossy."

All of Franklin's friends nodded.

"Bear's right," they said.

Franklin turned his back and went home.

There was no one to play with and nothing much to do. So, he helped his father all afternoon. They weeded the garden and washed the floors. And they made supper for Mole because he was sick.

"You're a good friend," Mole told Franklin's father.

On the way home, Franklin asked, "Do you and Mole have fights?"

"Sometimes," said Franklin's father. "But we always make up."

Franklin played alone for another whole day.
He missed Bear and all his friends. And he had
lots of time to think.
He would go to Bear and apologize.
Franklin and Bear met on the bridge.

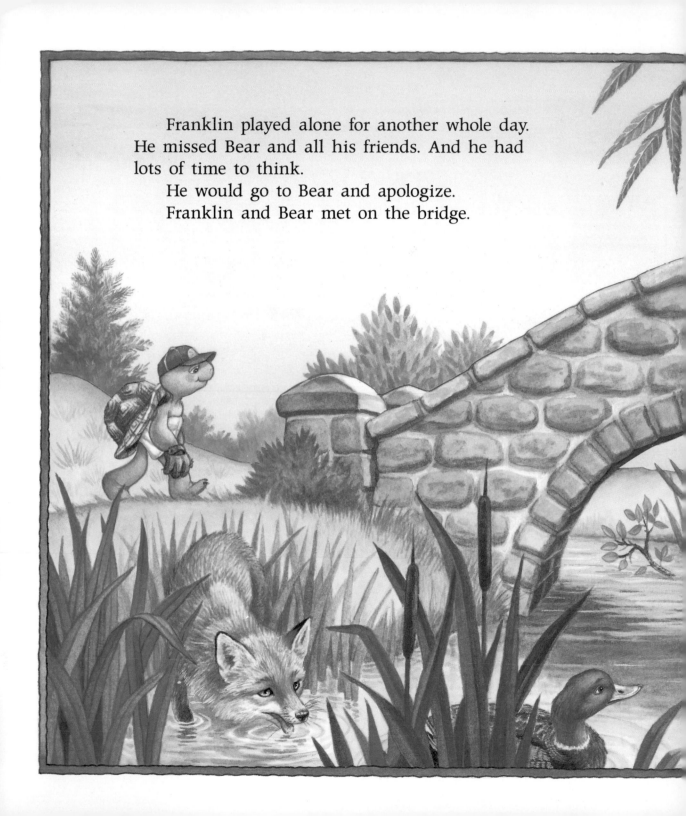

"I was going to your house," said Franklin.
"And I was going to your house," said Bear.
"I'm sorry," said Franklin. "It was all my fault."
"No, it was my fault," said Bear.
"Mine," said Franklin.
"No, mine," said Bear.

"STOP!" shouted Beaver, who was listening under the bridge.

"This is silly!" Beaver slapped her tail so hard that Franklin and Bear jumped. They started to giggle.

"Friends?" asked Franklin.
"Friends," said Bear.

Beaver wanted to play baseball. Bear and Goose and Duck agreed. They were picking teams when Franklin insisted on being the pitcher ... again.

All together his friends shouted, "No fair, Franklin!"

Franklin knew they were right. He couldn't always be pitcher. It was his turn to play in the outfield.

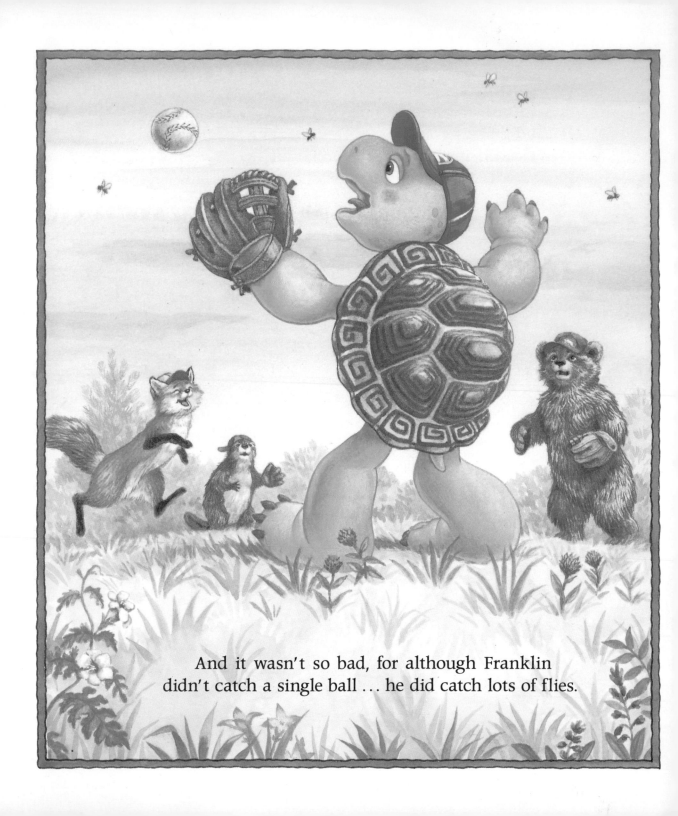

And it wasn't so bad, for although Franklin
didn't catch a single ball ... he did catch lots of flies.